Park Life

Emmanuelle Smith and Cally Lathey

Park Life ISBN 978-0-9930773-4-0
Fisherton Press Ltd

www.fishertonpress.co.uk

First published in 2016 in the United Kingdom

Text © Emmanuelle Smith 2016
Illustrations © Cally Lathey 2016

ISBN 978-0-9930773-4-0
A CIP catalogue record for this book is available from the British Library

It's dark in the park,
Quite early one morning.

The sun rising,
To warm the world.

Dogs and their walkers,
Early risers.

Time for
work,

Time for school.

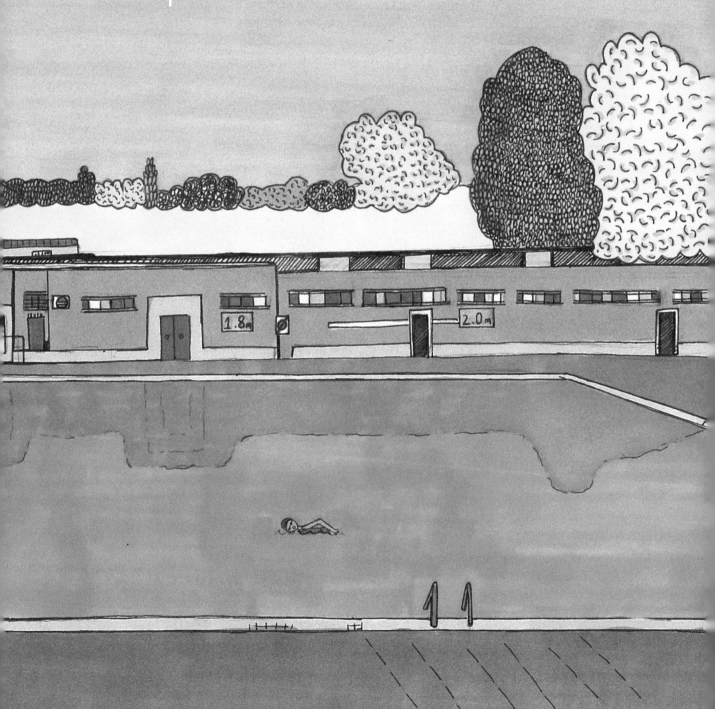

Time for a swim,
In the pool.

Time for a walk,

Take in the view.

A cup of tea.
Lunch outdoors.

Feed the ducks,
Pigeons, sparrows.

After school,
Relax and play.

Work is over,
For the day.

Swinging, sandpit,
Seesaw, slide.

Have a sit, a chat, a listen.

Sunset... Twilight... Dusk...

It's dark in the park,
Quite late, one night.

Inspired by:

John Donne - The Sun Rising

Dylan Thomas - Quite Early One Morning

Blur - Parklife

Brockwell Park

ES - For Rosa and Noam

CL - For Paddy

If you enjoyed this book...

Tell:

• your local librarian

• your teacher

• your friends

• your local bookshop

Write:

• to us general@fishertonpress.co.uk

• blog about it

• on social media #FishertonPress

• review it online

Buy:

• a copy for a friend

• birthday presents

• other Fisherton books

• and donate a book via our website

www.fishertonpress.co.uk

Lightning Source UK Ltd.
Milton Keynes UK
UKHW05f0630171018
330690UK00001B/12/P